TIME HUNTERS

PIRATE MUTINY

First published in Great Britain by HarperCollins *Children's Books* in 2014
HarperCollins *Children's Books* is a division of HarperCollins*Publishers* Ltd,
77–85 Fulham Palace Road, Hammersmith, London, W6 8JB.

The HarperCollins website address is: www.harpercollins.co.uk

1

Text © Hothouse Fiction Limited, 2014
Illustrations © HarperCollins *Children's Books*, 2014
Illustrations by Dynamo

ISBN 978-0-00-751406-9

Printed and bound in England by Clays Ltd, St Ives plc.

Conditions of Sale
This book is sold subject to the condition that it shall not, by way of trade
or otherwise, be lent, re-sold, hired out or otherwise circulated without
the publisher's prior consent in any form, binding or cover other than that
in which it is published and without a similar condition including this
condition being imposed on the subsequent purchaser. All rights reserved.

MIX
Paper from
responsible sources
FSC™ C007454

FSC™ is a non-profit international organisation established to promote
the responsible management of the world's forests. Products carrying the
FSC label are independently certified to assure consumers that they come
from forests that are managed to meet the social, economic and
ecological needs of present and future generations,
and other controlled sources.

Find out more about HarperCollins and the environment at
www.harpercollins.co.uk/green

CHRIS BLAKE

TIME HUNTERS

PIRATE MUTINY

HarperCollins *Children's Books*

Travel through time with Tom on more

adventures!

Gladiator Clash
Knight Quest
Viking Raiders
Greek Warriors
Pirate Mutiny
Egyptian Curse

Coming Soon!
Cowboy Showdown
Samurai Assassin
Outback Outlaw
Stone Age Rampage
Mohican Brave
Aztec Attack

For games, competitions and more visit:
www.time-hunters.com

CONTENTS

With special thanks to
Marnie Stanton-Riches

PROLOGUE

Five thousand years ago

Princess Isis and her pet cat, Cleo, stood outside the towering carved gates to the Afterlife. It had been rotten luck to fall off a pyramid and die at only ten years of age, but Isis wasn't worried – the Afterlife was meant to be great. People were dying to go there, after all! Her mummy's wrappings were so uncomfortable she couldn't wait a second longer to get in, get her body back and wear normal clothes again.

"Oi, Aaanuuubis, Anubidooby!" Isis shouted impatiently. "When you're ready, you old dog!"

Cleo started to claw Isis's shoulder. Then she yowled, jumping from Isis's arms and cowering behind her legs.

"Calm down, fluffpot," Isis said, bending to stroke her pet. "He can't exactly woof me to death!" The princess laughed, but froze when she stood up. Now she understood what Cleo had been trying to tell her.

Looming up in front of her was the enormous jackal-headed god of the Underworld himself, Anubis. He was so tall that Isis's neck hurt to look up at him. He glared down his long snout at her with angry red eyes. There was nothing pet-like about him. Isis gulped.

"'WHEN
YOU'RE READY,
YOU OLD DOG?'" Anubis
growled. "'ANUBIDOOBY?'"

Isis gave the god of the Underworld
a winning smile and held out five shining
amulets. She had been buried with them so
she could give them to Anubis to gain entry
to the Afterlife. There was a sixth amulet too
– a gorgeous green one. But Isis had hidden
it under her arm. Green *was* her favourite
colour, and surely Anubis didn't need all six.

Except the god didn't seem to agree. His fur bristled in rage. "FIVE? Where is the sixth?" he demanded.

Isis shook her head. "I was only given five," she said innocently.

To her horror, Anubis grabbed the green amulet from its hiding place. "You little LIAR!" he bellowed.

Thunder started to rumble. The ground shook. Anubis snatched all six amulets and tossed them into the air. With a loud crack and a flash of lightning, they vanished.

"You hid them from me!" he boomed. "Now I have hidden them from you – in the most dangerous places throughout time."

Isis's bandaged shoulders drooped in despair. "So I c-c-can't come into the Afterlife then?"

"Not until you have found each and every

one. But first, you will have to get out of this..." Anubis clicked his fingers. A life-sized pottery statue of the goddess Isis, whom Isis was named after, appeared before him.

Isis felt herself being sucked into the statue, along with Cleo. "What are you doing to me?" she yelled.

"You can only escape if somebody breaks the statue," Anubis said. "So you'll have plenty of time to think about whether trying to trick the trickster god himself was a good idea!"

The walls of the statue closed around Isis, trapping her and Cleo inside. The sound of Anubis's evil laughter would be the last sound they would hear for a long, long time...

CHAPTER 1
ISIS MAKES A SPLASH

"Tom! Are you listening?" a deep voice shouted. "Or maybe you're too busy talking to yourself?"

Tom looked up at his swimming instructor. His face was red. His T-shirt was red. Even the knobbly knees sticking out from under his shorts were red. "I am listening, sir."

"Four lengths, front crawl," the instructor said, swinging his arms in big circles to show the correct technique.

Tom nodded and tried to stop his teeth from chattering. He caught a glimpse of Princess Isis Amun-Ra standing by the poolside with her cat, Cleo. The Ancient Egyptian mummy was cheekily swinging her arms round, imitating Tom's swimming teacher.

"And Tom," the instructor said, "next length, *keep your head in the water!*"

Tom clung to the side of the pool, shivering as the cold water lapped over his ears.

"I really wish I could go for a swim," Isis said, standing with her toes curled over the edge of the tiles. "You're so lucky. I *love* swimming."

"No! Don't even think about it," Tom said. "Your bandages will get all soggy." He gulped at the thought. "The pool's yucky enough as it is. And what would you do with

Cleo? She hates water!"

"Alice, go! Veejay, go! Tom, go!" the instructor shouted.

Tom pushed himself forward and started to swim down the lane. Every time he lifted his head to the side to gasp for air, he could see Isis strutting along beside him, holding her mummified cat.

"That's right, Tom! Kick your legs!" she shouted.

Tom put his head back in the water. *I'm so glad nobody else can see or hear her,* he thought. *She's so embarrassing!*

Two strokes later, he came up for air again.

"You're too slow!" Isis yelled.

When his instructor was looking the other way, Tom started to tread water. He glared up at Isis.

14

"Who made you a swimming expert?" he said.

Isis held Cleo to her chest and put one hand on her hip. "I learned to swim in the River Nile, I'll have you know," she said. "And if I'd swum as slowly as you do, I'd have been eaten by the crocodiles!"

"Oh, really?" Tom said, pushing his wet hair out of his eyes. "Well, why don't you just go back to Ancient Egypt and jump in the Nile right now?"

Isis let out a sigh of irritation. "I would if I could," she said. "It's your fault that I'm here!" She pointed a finger at him. "You were the one who smashed the statue and released me and Cleo!"

"Yes, but it was your attitude that got you stuck in the statue in the first place," Tom said. "The fact that you can't get into the

15

Afterlife until you've found the amulets has nothing to do with me. I just got roped into all this by accident!"

"Tom! No slacking!" the instructor's gruff voice echoed across the pool. "Backstroke now!"

Tom turned over and started to swim on his back. He looked up at the ceiling, trying to ignore the mummy walking along the edge of the pool.

Suddenly, Tom was hit in the nose by something spongy.

"Aargh!" he yelped.

Next, he was hit in the shoulder. Isis was standing beside a stack of swimming floats. One by one, she hurled them at Tom. They hit the water with a *plop*!

Breeet! The instructor's whistle piped shrilly across the pool area.

"Oi! Tom!" he boomed. "No floats allowed."

Tom gulped. *Great*, he thought. *It's always the same. Isis gets me into trouble wherever we go.* He flung one of the floats back at Isis. But the mummified princess merely ducked and giggled.

As Tom finished his length, the water in the pool started to get choppy. Tom spluttered as he swallowed a mouthful of water.

He looked round to see who was splashing. But the other children in his class had already climbed out. All by itself, the pool was churning and bubbling like a witch's cauldron.

An enormous wave rose up out of the centre of the pool. It curled over Tom's head and came crashing down.

Isis and Cleo clambered up the lifeguard's chair to safety.

"What's going on?" Tom cried.

"It's Anubis!" she yelped. "Who else would try to drown us?"

CRASH! Another wave slapped down. Tom bobbed up and down in the water, fighting to keep his head above the surface. *Oh, no,* he thought. *I don't want to go time travelling*

now! I'm all wet!

The water in the centre of the pool swelled higher and higher, until two pointed ears broke through the surface. Then two glowing red eyes appeared, followed by a giant black snout. It was Anubis, the Ancient Egyptian god of the Underworld. He had the giant body of a man, but the head of a jackal.

"Hello, you little water rats," Anubis bellowed. "Are you ready for your next adventure?"

"I'm pretty sure dogs aren't allowed in the swimming pool," Isis called from the lifeguard's chair.

Anubis shook his head from side to side like a wet dog, spraying drops of water. "I see you're still as disrespectful as ever," he growled at her. "So I'm going to send you to someone who will teach you a lesson or two!"

Tom scrambled out of the pool and stood on the edge shivering.

As Anubis disappeared back under the surface in a funnel of water, it looked like somebody had yanked a plug out of the pool.

An icy wind whipped up round Tom, Isis and Cleo. Tom felt himself being pulled through the tunnels of time.

"I wonder where we're going?" Isis shouted, as they sped along.

"I don't know, but we're about to find out!" called Tom.

CHAPTER 2
SUN, SEA... AND SALMAGUNDI

"Wheeeeeeee!" Tom cried with delight, wondering where they would land. Anubis had hidden Isis's amulets in some amazing – but dangerous – places and times. They'd found the last one in Ancient Greece, and before that they'd travelled back to Viking times, medieval England and Ancient Rome. There were only two more amulets to find now, and Tom couldn't wait to see where the next one would be.

The three time travellers shot out of the tunnel and tumbled through warm air. They landed on fine white sand with a *flump*.

"Ooooh," Isis cooed. "Look!" She stretched out an arm and pointed to the horizon.

Tom squinted at her in the blinding sunlight. "What? You've got your normal body back?" he asked. "No surprise there! That always happens when we travel through time."

Isis shook her head. "No, silly! I'm talking about where we are." She waved her arm around. "It's gorgeous!"

It was true. They had landed on a perfect sandy beach in a deserted bay. Palm trees heavy with coconuts nodded in a light sea breeze. The blue sea lapped gently against the sand.

23

She's right, Tom thought, chuckling to himself. *This place isn't bad. Maybe Anubis has sent us on a tropical holiday.*

Tom looked down at his linen shirt and baggy breeches. "Look! My trunks have gone!" he said.

Isis tugged at her clothes. "What are these ridiculous outfits, exactly?" she asked.

Tom felt the frill on his shirt. "Not sure," he said, frowning. "I don't like the girly ruffles, though."

Isis lay back on the warm sand with her arms behind her head. She looked at Tom with sparkling brown eyes that were lined with kohl. "This sunshine is just like being back home in Egypt," she said, sighing happily. "So much nicer than cold and rainy old Britain. Never mind the Afterlife. Let's just stay here! We can relax all day long and

24

eat fresh fish and drink coconut milk!"

Cleo mewed in agreement before running off to chase crabs.

Tom leaped up. "Not a chance," he said. "Come on! Let's go exploring!"

After an hour of wandering in the hot sun, Isis didn't seem to be enjoying the heat any more.

"I'm thirsty," she moaned, grabbing her throat. "You *have* to find me some water."

But as the three of them came out of a cove, Isis suddenly fell silent. Tom stared at the row of shop fronts and inns that lined the next bay along. They were all painted in pretty pastel colours. In the distance, people hurried along the promenade.

"I wonder what kind of place this is?" Isis said.

Tom gazed out to where large ships were anchored in the deeper water. Suddenly he spotted their flags, showing skulls, crossbones and cutlasses.

"Pirates!" he gulped.

Isis's eyes widened. "Pirates?" she asked,

raising an eyebrow. "We had those back in my day."

"I'm pretty sure we're not in Ancient Egypt," said Tom. He sheltered his eyes from the glare of the sun with his hand. "Those ships look like French or Dutch galleons," he

said. "I've seen them in books and films."

Tom was about to ask Isis if she had ever seen *Pirates of the Caribbean*, but he realised how silly that would sound to someone who had lived five thousand years ago.

"So where are we?" Isis asked, as she scratched Cleo behind the ears.

"I think we're in the eighteenth century," Tom said. "Pirates were a massive problem then. They were always attacking ships carrying things like gold."

"Gold?" Isis asked, wide-eyed.

"You bet!" Tom said. "The Caribbean Sea was where all the big pirate battles happened."

"How could anyone want to fight when they're living here?" Isis said, looking at the beautiful view.

"Forget the scenery!" Tom said. "We need to ask your scarab ring for some help if we're going to find the fifth amulet."

Isis nodded and stroked the magical golden scarab that sat on her finger. On it was a picture of the goddess Isis, whom Isis was named after. The ring had given Tom and Isis clues about where the first four amulets were hidden. "Goddess Isis," Isis began. "Please, please help us once more! Tell us where we can find the fifth amulet."

Silvery words flew up out of the ring and hung in the air in a riddle. Tom read it out to Isis:

"To seek this jewel, shining greeny-blue,
In a Spaniard's chest of bullion,
First you must join the ragged crew,
As the Teacher's lowly scullion.
His whiskers threaten like a thundercloud,
He's the high seas' worst rapscallion,

29

But he'll help you pinch it from the crab,
Within sight of the red cross galleon."

Isis sighed. "I haven't got a clue what any of that means," she said. "I never do. Explain, Professor Smartypants!"

"Well, it mentions a Spaniard," Tom said. "Most of the Caribbean islands were ruled by the Spanish. Not sure about the rest, but it sounds like we've got to look for a man with a hairy, scary face! Maybe the red cross means we'll find him at a hospital."

Tom, Isis and Cleo set off walking towards the busy harbour.

"What's a 'rapscallion'?" Isis asked.

"My grandad uses that word," Tom said. "I think it means that we're after a bad guy."

Before they'd gone far, they crossed paths with a young man. He was running so fast, he almost crashed right into them.

"Watch it!" Tom said.

The young man adjusted the red scarf that was tied round his long, dark hair. He wore the same kind of breeches and shirt as Tom and Isis, except his were covered in stains.

"Sorry!" he said, frowning. "What's a pair of nippers doing in a dangerous hole like New Providence?"

"Is that where we are?" Tom asked. He had heard about New Providence in his history books. It was a famous pirate port.

The young man nodded. "Of course! You two need to get yourselves home sharpish, before you run into trouble."

"Oh, we can't," Tom said, thinking fast. "We've been, er… shipwrecked. Our parents were lost at sea, but we clung to some wood and floated to this island."

31

Isis pulled a sad face and sniffed, adding, "We don't have a home to go back to…"

The young man held out his hand. "Salmagundi's the name. Sal for short. I'm sorry to hear about your troubles."

Tom shook Sal's hand. "I'm Tom, this is Isis, and her cat, Cleo."

"Listen," Sal said, leaning in. His tanned face made his green eyes look slightly wild. "Not everyone here on New Providence is nice. So stick by me, OK? I'll take you to the Jolly Barnacle Inn. I do the cooking there. But one day I'm going to be a pirate."

Tom and Isis exchanged excited glances.

Sal straightened up and peered at the sun. "But we'd better hurry, because if I don't get a move on, I'll be getting fifty of the owner's best."

"Best what?" Isis asked.

"Fifty lashes. With a whip!"

"Ouch!" said Isis, wincing.

As Tom, Isis and Cleo followed Sal into the port, Tom saw that the row of shops wasn't very pretty close up. There was broken glass in the window frames and rotten vegetables all over the ground.

"Eeew!" he said to Isis. "What a pong."

Isis nodded, holding her shirt over her nose.

They arrived at the Jolly Barnacle Inn, with its sign hung crookedly over the door. As soon as they stepped inside, a finely

dressed pirate with the most rotten teeth Tom
had ever seen hurled a bar stool at another
mean-looking, muscly man.

"Are you sayin' I look like a girl?" the
elegant pirate said. He cocked his pistol and
fired it at the ceiling, so
that plaster showered
down.

The muscly pirate
laughed heartily.
"You look so much
like a woman, they
won't let you back
on your own ship
with the *real* men!"
He smacked the
pistol out of the first
pirate's hand.
"I'll slit your gizzard

for that!" the first pirate cried, drawing his cutlass.

Crumbs, Tom thought. *Talk about overreacting.*

Tom, Isis, Cleo and Sal edged past the fighting pair.

"Never insult a pirate if you value your life," Sal advised them.

Sal led them to an empty table in the corner. "Sit here, and try to stay out of everyone's way," he said. "I'll find you a little something to eat."

As Sal disappeared into the kitchen, Isis looked round and wrinkled her nose.

"This place is disgusting," she said loudly. She poked the tabletop and shuddered. "Yuck. It's *sticky*."

"Then don't touch it!" Tom said.

"This place isn't fit for a princess!" Isis protested.

35

"Keep your voice down," Tom whispered. "I'm not sure these pirates would take kindly to you insulting their favourite hang-out."

Sal returned and slammed two tankards down on the table. "Grog," he announced. "Drink up!"

Tom sipped the drink... and immediately spat it out.

"Ugh! Sal, what do they put in this? Washing-up liquid?" he cried.

"No idea what you're talking about, shipmate. It'll put hairs on your chest."

Sal swigged the contents of his tankard. Grog poured down the sides of his chin and on to his shirt. Then he went back to work in the kitchen.

Pretending to drink, Tom and Isis listened to what was being said by a scary-looking group of pirates at the next table.

"So, Jones tells me there be a Spanish merchant ship leaving Cuba," one man said, glancing round to make sure no one else was listening.

"What's it carrying?" another asked, scratching his nose with his dagger hilt. "Will there be rum and spices and sugar and—"

"Aye," the first man said, nodding. "And cotton too. But listen..." He looked round again, then whispered, "It's got a chest full of gold!"

"Ooooooh!" the other pirates gasped.

Tom was just about to nudge Isis when there was a crash, followed by gunshots. Tom turned round and saw a huge, fearsome man standing in the doorway pointing a gun into the room. He had the biggest, blackest beard Tom had ever seen. His bushy whiskers were plaited with colourful ribbons at the end. Tom gulped.

Suddenly, every man in the inn started screaming as loud bangs, pops and flashes of light exploded round the man.

"We're under attack!" Sal yelled.

Tom dived to the floor and pulled Isis down with him. A terrified Cleo leaped into Isis's arms.

"Under the table – quick!" Tom said.

As he, Isis and Cleo hid beneath the table, another explosion went off with a terrifying BANG!

CHAPTER 3
A SCARY TEACHER

Tom sniffed the air. He recognised the smell from Bonfire Night parties. The explosions coming out of the pirate's beard were just fireworks! The thought of bangers suddenly jogged his memory.

"Remember your ring told us about the rapscallion with thundercloud whiskers?" Tom whispered to Isis. "Well, if I'm not wrong, that dangerous-looking pirate over there is none other than the legendary Blackbeard!"

"Blackbeard?" Isis asked, frowning.

"Yep. The one and only," Tom said, barely able to contain his excitement. "His real name was Edward Teach. In the riddle, it mentioned a Teacher. Get it? Teacher… Teach!"

"Yessss!" Isis snapped. "I may be dead but I'm not stupid! So why's he such a legend?"

"He was one of the most famous pirates ever." Tom explained. "He used fireworks to scare other sailors."

"Well, that sort of trick doesn't work on me," Isis said.

Tom raised his eyebrow. "That's funny – you looked pretty scared when you dived under the table with me," he said. "Anyway, Blackbeard was a really successful pirate, stealing gold, medicine, weapons and other valuables from ships in the West Indies."

40

"And we've got to join his crew so that we can find the amulet?" Isis chewed nervously on her bottom lip.

Tom nodded. "Yup. That's what the riddle says."

Just then, Blackbeard shot a hole in the ceiling and leaped up on to the bar. The other pirates cowered in fear, holding their tankards to their chests like tin teddy bears.

"Listen up, you mangy lot!" Blackbeard barked. He stroked his beard and glared down at everyone. "I'm searching for the roughest, toughest crew to ever sail the high seas! My men have got to be as strong as iron and hard as nails!"

Just then, Sal returned to the table. He was carrying two large bowls.

"Here you go, me hearties!" he said, slamming the bowls down. "Salmagundi. I'm

41

nicknamed after this dish!"

Tom peered into the bowl. He could see
a stew of meat, eggs and gravy on a bed of
lettuce, and there was a whiff of fish coming
from the dish. He was just about to ask Sal
what kind of hideous food this was when—

"I'm so hungry I could eat a whale!"
Blackbeard's voice shook the inn. "Where
can I get some grub?"

Tom thought quickly. This was their
chance to meet Blackbeard!

"Here, sir!" He shouted to the fearsome
pirate captain. "You can have my
salmagundi!"

Blackbeard jumped down from the bar, his
coat-tails flapping. He stomped over to them.
Grabbing the spoon out of Tom's bowl,
Blackbeard slurped the strange stew in one
long gulp.

"Thanks, lad," he said, wiping away a dribble running down one of his beard-ribbons. "That's the best salmagundi I've ever tasted."

Isis snorted and whispered, "His tastebuds must be deader than mine!"

Tom nudged her in the ribs.

"Who cooked up this feast?" Blackbeard demanded.

Tom pointed to Sal. "Our friend Sal did," he said.

Blackbeard licked the spoon and dropped it back in the bowl with a clatter. "My ship needs a new cook. The old one's got a hook for his hand now and isn't much use in the galley." Blackbeard slapped a giant hand on Sal's shoulder. "You're hired!"

Sal's face lit up. "What an honour, sir," he said, beaming.

With a flourish, the pirate captain unsheathed his cutlass and turned to the other men at the inn.

"Now, which of you devil's dogs fancy

working aboard my ship?" he boomed. "Come and fight me if you think you're up to it!"

One by one, hopeful pirates started to duel with Blackbeard. Their cutlasses clashed and clanged. Tables were upturned. Chairs were smashed against the inn's walls.

"You're hired!" Blackbeard said to the men who fought skilfully.

"Get out, you harbour rats!" he said to the men who couldn't match him. "Don't show your face here again!"

"Why are they all so keen to join his crew?" Isis asked. "He doesn't seem very nice."

Tom nodded. "True, but being a pirate must have been easier than being an ordinary sailor – and they got a lot more money."

Isis stroked Cleo thoughtfully. "Well, it's

all very well sitting here and watching this lot," she said. "But *we've* got to get on board Blackbeard's ship somehow."

Tom nodded. "Yes, the riddle said something about being a lowly scullion." He turned to Sal, who was picking at his teeth with a fishbone. "What's a scullion, Sal?"

"Kitchen helper. Sweeper-upper. General dogsbody," he said.

Isis shook her head. "I will not be a dogsbody for *anyone*," she said.

Eyes flashing, she marched straight over to Blackbeard and tugged on one of his beard-ribbons. "Me and my friend here want to join your crew," she announced brightly.

Blackbeard peered down at her with beady black eyes. After a moment, he threw his head back, laughing. "I'm no babysitter, little lad," he said, patting Isis on the head.

"I am NOT a little—"

Tom shot Isis a warning look before she could tell Blackbeard that she was a girl.

"—lad," she continued indignantly. "I am a VERY strong and brave lad."

Blackbeard looked unconvinced.

Tom could feel their chance slipping away. *I have to say something*, he thought.

"And I'm really good at geography," he told Blackbeard. "I can help you navigate."

Isis pushed Tom out of the way. "I'm good at just about everything," she said. "Come on! Duel with me!" She grabbed a broken chair leg off the sticky floor and whacked Blackbeard on the arm with it.

Blackbeard growled.

Oh, no, Tom thought. *Isis is going to get us into trouble again!*

"Stop your jibber jabber or you'll taste the

back of my sword!" Blackbeard roared. He grabbed Tom and Isis by their collars and shoved them out on to the street. "You're too young to be pirates, anyhow!" he growled, slamming the door shut.

Tom, Isis and Cleo wandered round New Providence trying to think of a plan. If they didn't get on board Blackbeard's boat, they would never find the amulet or get home again. After their visit to the Jolly Barnacle, Tom no longer thought New Providence was a tropical paradise – and he didn't want to be stuck there forever!

"We've got to find Sal," Tom said. "I bet he can help us."

They found Sal at the port, loading crates of limes on to a ship. Its name, which was painted on the bow, was *Queen Anne's Revenge*.

Isis snorted. "It doesn't look much, does it?" she said. "It's just a tiny sailing boat next to those big galleons."

"Ho there, little shipmates!" Sal said, puffing and panting as he rolled a barrel up the gangplank. "The *Queen Anne's Revenge* is a sloop. This little lady will outrun and outgun any other ship on the high seas," he explained.

Tom looked up at its flag, flapping merrily above the crow's nest.

In one hand, a skeleton held an hourglass. In its other hand was a spear. Next to it was a bleeding heart.

Yikes, Tom thought, gulping hard. *That's not very welcoming. But we've got to get on board, no matter what.*

He took a deep breath and started to help Sal roll the barrel up the gangplank.

"Can you help us stow away on the ship?" he whispered to Sal.

Isis trotted after them, holding a very nervous Cleo. "Please? We really need to get on board," she begged.

Sal scratched his head. "I don't know about that," he said. "I'll get into boiling water if Blackbeard finds out I'm hiding stowaways."

"If we get caught we won't tell anyone it was you who let us on," Isis said.

"Come on, Sal. We helped you get this job, didn't we?" Tom said. "And we promise to stand by you if you get in trouble."

50

He saluted. "Pirate's honour!"

Sal groaned. "Oh, go on then!" he said. Checking that nobody was watching, he led them back down to the loading bay, where he found an empty rum barrel. "Get in – I'll roll you into the hold."

As the barrel rumbled on to the wooden deck, making Tom feel like he was on a bumpy funfair ride, Isis sneezed.

"Shh!" Sal whispered. "Sneezing as you board a ship is bad luck! Even a landlubber should know that much."

After Sal left them in the hold, Tom, Isis and Cleo huddled in the dark barrel, which smelled of rum and oak.

"This is no better than being in that nasty statue, is it, Fluffpot?" Isis said to Cleo.

"Be quiet!" Tom hissed. "We don't want to get caught, remember?"

Tom could hear heavy footsteps thumping above him as the pirates boarded the ship and prepared to set sail. Then there was a clanking sound that he guessed was the anchor being hauled up the side of the ship. Not long after, the *Queen Anne's Revenge* started to rise and fall.

"I feel sick," Isis wailed.

Cleo yowled in agreement.

"I think we can get out now," Tom said. "The ship has definitely left port."

Checking there was no one else about, they climbed out of the barrel, stretching and taking deep breaths until they found their sea legs. On all sides, crates and barrels were stacked high.

"Let's have a look round," said Isis. "Maybe we'll find the treasure chest with the amulet inside before anyone finds us!"

Tom started to poke about inside the crates as quietly as he could. "There's plenty of guns and ammunition, but no treasure," he said, holding his nose as he peered into another container. "I think this is salted pork. Pooooooeey! It doesn't smell like anything I'd want to eat."

Isis leaned into a barrel that was labelled 'Hard Tack'.

"There are some really tough biscuits in here," she said, trying to break one in half. She rummaged in another barrel and accidentally knocked over a thick coil of rope. It fell to the floor with a thud.

"Shh!" hissed Tom. "We don't want to get caught."

"Maybe we should try looking on the upper decks?" suggested Isis.

They tiptoed up the stairs. With every

squeak, Tom's heart pounded. Looking round to check that the coast was clear, they explored the sleeping quarters. They found hammocks hanging from the ceiling, but there was no sign of the amulet. On the gun deck, there was a lot of cannons, but no treasure chest in sight.

"Nothing!" Tom muttered.

"We'll have to search the main deck," Isis said.

Tom paused and listened to the stamping of the pirates' boots on the deck overhead.

"What are you waiting for?" Isis demanded impatiently.

Tom gulped as he remembered Blackbeard's terrifying behaviour in the Jolly Barnacle. Maybe it would be safer to wait until dark to explore there?

But Isis had already started up the stairs.

Following behind her, Tom emerged on the main deck and breathed in the fresh sea air. Glancing over the side of the boat, he saw foamy lines trailing in the ship's wake. Above him, rigging stretched upwards, making the *Revenge* look like it was a spider's web.

A voice shouted, "Gather round, me hearties!"

Tom, Isis and Cleo quickly ducked behind some crates as the pirates gathered on the deck.

"There's the captain!" Tom said, nodding at Blackbeard.

The entire crew was assembled before him.

"Right! You new fellers need to meet my old hands," he boomed. He pointed to a tall, fierce-looking man who stepped forward. Blackbeard slapped a hand on his back. "This hawk-eyed meanie is Little Jack. He escaped from the British navy, no less. He's my quartermaster."

Next, Blackbeard pointed to a dark-skinned man who was short and stocky. "This here's Silas. Once a slave. Now my carpenter."

Blackbeard pushed a man with an eye patch forward. "Meet One-eye Pete, my gunner," he said. "Fancies himself as a joker, don't you, shipmate?"

One-eye Pete lifted his patch up. "Eye, eye, Captain! Geddit?!"

Finally Blackbeard paced the deck, explaining the ship's rules to the crew. The punishments for breaking any of the rules sounded terrifying: walking the plank, being flogged with a cat-o'-nine tails, being marooned on an island, or – worst of all – keelhauling, which involved being dragged

underwater over the razor-sharp barnacles
clinging to the ship's keel.

*Ouch! I don't fancy getting on the wrong side of
Blackbeard,* thought a trembling Tom.

"The sooner we find the amulet and get back, the better," Tom whispered to Isis.

Suddenly familiar laughter boomed round the deck.

"Anubis!" whispered Tom.

The enormous god of the Underworld rose up on the deck of the ship. "You're not going home any time soon!" he roared.

Anubis leaped into the air, then jumped into the water below, sending a huge wave crashing into the side of the ship. *Queen Anne's Revenge* rocked back and forth like a see-saw. The crates slid away, leaving Tom, Isis and Cleo in plain view.

Blackbeard sprinted over to them, a fierce look on his face. He grabbed them by their collars. "You again!" he bellowed.

CHAPTER 4

SHARK BAIT

"Spies!" Blackbeard barked in Tom's face. "Only spies would be stupid enough to stow away on board my ship! Who are you working for?"

Tom caught a whiff of Sal's stew on the ferocious pirate's breath. He wrinkled his nose, wishing Blackbeard would put him and Isis down.

"Who sent you here?" Blackbeard snarled. "The French? The Spanish?"

"We're not spies!" Isis said. "The Egyptian god of the Underworld himself sent us here, you big, beardy barnacle. Now, get your hands off me, will you?"

Blackbeard's eyebrows bunched together. "What a load of codswallop! Are you trying to mock me?"

Tom's heart was thudding so hard, he thought it might break through his ribs.

"W-we're telling the truth," Tom said. "Honest. We're absolutely, positively *not* spies."

The huge pirate snorted. "You must think I'm a fool. Well, Blackbeard is no numbskull!"

Tucking Tom under one arm and Isis under the other, the pirate captain strode to the side of the ship. "Ready the plank, Little Jack!" he barked. "I've had enough of our

uninvited guests. Let's see if the waves can wash the lies out of them!"

"What's happening?" Isis cried, as One-eye Pete tied their hands behind their backs.

"Time to walk the plank, lads!" he said, giving Isis a rough shove.

A narrow wooden plank jutted out over the waves. Tom caught sight of Isis's face – for once his brave friend looked absolutely terrified. Cleo leaped on to her mistress's shoulder and wrapped herself round Isis's neck like a scarf.

Tom glanced round the ship, desperately looking for an escape route. Could he make a break for it and shimmy up the mast? Not with his hands tied…

"I'll go first, shall I?" Tom offered.

Isis blinked hard. "Y–yes. Maybe just this once," she said, giving him a grateful smile and stepping back on to the safety of the deck.

"As soon as you hit the water, kick your legs like mad and try to get your wrists free," Tom whispered.

"I'll just pretend I'm swimming in the Nile," Isis said bravely.

Feeling the tip of Blackbeard's sheathed dagger poke in his back, Tom took a step on to the plank. "That's right," Blackbeard said. "One foot in front of the other!"

Tom wobbled along the plank. It reminded him of the diving board at the pool where he had his swimming lessons. He hated the way it boinged up and down, like it was trying to tip the children off on purpose.

Be brave. Show no fear, so Isis doesn't get too scared, he thought, trying to keep himself calm as his teeth chattered with fear.

Looking down, Tom saw the sea churning below him. Sticking out of the water were five grey triangles.

"Sharks!" he whimpered. They were swimming in a circle, as if they knew they were about to be served a tasty lunch of two children and a cat.

64

"Some use all those swimming lessons were!" Tom muttered, as he shuffled to the end of the plank. "Even the best front crawl in the world won't save me now!"

Tom looked out at the horizon for what he was fairly certain was the last time, and gulped. He was definitely out of ideas now.

"A ship!" he gasped.

Sure enough, a tall ship was sailing towards the sloop at great speed. *It's heading right at us,* Tom thought.

He looked back at Blackbeard and his crew. Had they noticed? But they were only watching him and Isis.

"Hey! Look! There's a ship coming!" Tom shouted.

Blackbeard whipped out a telescope from his coat. He extended it and peered at the approaching ship that was flying the American flag.

"Shiver me timbers!" he said. Lowering his telescope, he stared grimly at the crew. "It's the *Sweet Caroline*! The governor of North Carolina is after me!"

"Why's that, Captain?" one of the new crew members asked.

Blackbeard tugged at his beard and smirked. "He hasn't forgiven me for raiding ships in Charleston harbour! All hands on deck! Let's give *Sweet Caroline* a run for her money!"

Blackbeard looked up at Tom, wobbling on the plank.

"You're in luck, boy!" he barked. "You're not going to Davy Jones's Locker yet. You spotted the governor's ship, so you've proved yourself worthy. And I'm feeling generous, so

I'm going to let all three of you live!"

With a sigh of relief, Tom shuffled carefully along the plank, back towards the boat. Blackbeard cut them all loose.

"Where's Davy Jones's Locker?" Isis whispered to Tom, rubbing her wrists.

"It's the bottom of the sea – it's what pirates call drowning," Tom whispered back.

"Looks like I've got myself two cabin boys now," Blackbeard said. "And that cat had better be good at catching mice, because we're overrun with them."

Cleo meowed happily.

Soon, the *Sweet Caroline* was close behind the *Queen Anne's Revenge*. Blackbeard bellowed orders to his crew, while Tom and Isis wondered what to do.

BOOM! Suddenly Tom saw a puff of black smoke rise up from the governor's ship. A cannonball whizzed past the *Revenge*, narrowly missing the ship's bow. It hit the water – *splash!* – sending up a cloud of spray. Then came another. This time, the *Revenge* shuddered as the cannonball crashed into the side, splintering the wood.

"They're firing on us, Captain!" Silas shouted.

"Raise the sails!" Blackbeard ordered.

"HEAVE! HEAVE! HEAVE!" The men worked together, tugging at the ropes until the sails began to unfurl. Soon, the sails filled with wind and the *Revenge* picked up speed as it sailed away from the *Sweet Caroline*.

Little Jack, the quartermaster, shouted at Tom. "You, boy! Climb up to the crow's nest! We need a lookout."

Tom gazed up at the main mast. The crow's nest was so high up it looked like a small bucket.

"Who? Me?" he asked.

"Get up there," Little Jack growled. "Or you'll find yourself walking the plank again!"

Taking a deep breath, Tom started to climb the rigging. It swayed with every step he took.

"I'm going to die," Tom muttered, as he went higher and higher. "I survived the plank, but I'm still going to be eaten by sharks if I fall."

The ship lurched from one side to the other as it cut through the swelling waves.

Clinging on, Tom pulled himself into the crow's nest, which was a little platform surrounded by railings. From this lookout point, Tom could see that the *Sweet Caroline* was some way behind them now. Below, Blackbeard was wrestling with the ship's

wheel, as the *Revenge* powered ahead with the wind in its sails.

Tom forced himself to look down. The water had suddenly changed from deep blue to pale green. Just ahead a long strip of white sand poked through the water's surface.

"Land ho!" Tom cried. He closed his eyes as the *Revenge* thundered on towards it. "We're going to run aground!" he shouted down to the men below.

Tom crouched in the crow's nest and braced himself for the jolt that would surely come.

When the *Revenge* swung violently round to the right, Tom thought they had hit the sandbar. He peered over the edge of the crow's nest to see Blackbeard steering the ship into a tight turn. The crew cheered as the *Revenge* pulled away from the strip of land and tacked a safe course back into deeper waters.

But the *Sweet Caroline* was a much bigger ship. Tom could see its captain was trying to turn it round, but it was going too fast.

"Watch this, lads!" Blackbeard shouted gleefully.

The crew of the *Queen Anne's Revenge* leaned over the side and cheered as the other ship ploughed on to the sandbank. With a

nasty judder, it came to a standstill. Some of
the governor's crew lost their balance and
went splashing overboard, into the shallow
water.

"Enjoy your swim!" hooted One-eye Pete.

"You lot are shark bait now!" cackled
Little Jack.

"Safe from capture yet again!" Blackbeard
whooped as the *Revenge* fled.

Tom climbed down from the crow's nest.

Blackbeard, who was waiting at the
bottom, clapped a giant hand on his
shoulder. "We'll make a pirate out of you
yet, boy!" he said.

CHAPTER 5
PLAYING WITH ST ELMO'S FIRE

"Take this plate of hard tack to One-eye Pete," Sal said, thrusting a metal dish into Tom's hands. He passed another to Isis. "Give this one to Little Jack."

"Ugh!" Isis cried. She wrinkled her nose in disgust and held the plate away from her.

"Look lively!" Sal said.

Tom peered down at the tough biscuits. At first he thought they had nuts in them. Then he realised the nuts were crawling.

"Aargh! These biscuits are alive!" Tom said, dropping the plate.

Sal started to laugh. He picked up the tack and shoved the breakfast plate back into Tom's hands. "Weevils," he explained. "That's all. The hard tack gets full of them, because us pirates are at sea for so long. We have to use up the old food before starting on the fresh supplies."

Feeling slightly sick, Tom and Isis served the most important members of Blackbeard's crew. Once everyone was sitting on deck, gnawing on the hard, infested biscuits, Tom, Isis and Sal sat down.

Sal dropped

two hard biscuits on to their plates with a clatter. "There you go, me hearties! Fill your boots!"

A fat little weevil crept out of a hole in Tom's breakfast biscuit.

"I am NOT eating bugs," Tom said. He pushed his plate aside. *All the more reason to find the amulet fast*, he thought. *Otherwise I'll starve to death.*

Isis was picking the wriggling insects out of hers. "I'd rather *not* starve," she said. She lowered her voice to a whisper. "It's bad enough being dead without having a growling stomach."

Sal threw something small and green to Tom. Tom caught it and saw that it was a lime.

"Cut it in half and suck out the juice," Sal explained. "Come on, now, you have to do this!"

"Why?" Tom asked, sucking on the sour fruit.

"Scurvy, of course!" Sal said. "If you don't get your limes, all your teeth will drop out, you'll get covered in spots and your legs will swell up. Then you'll DIE!"

Isis glanced over at Cleo, who was stretched out on the deck in the morning sun, purring loudly.

"Lucky Fluffpot," she said. "Cleo's already caught a bellyful of mice this morning. She won't go hungry!"

After breakfast, Tom and Isis went below deck to find Silas.

Tom cleared his throat. "Er... hello," he said to the ship's carpenter. "Blackbeard told us to come and help you."

Silas was sawing away at a plank of

wood. The noise of the saw was so loud, Tom wondered if Silas had heard him. But then the carpenter looked up, wiped his sweaty brow and smiled.

"Welcome, shipmates!" Silas said, beckoning Tom and Isis closer. "I could use some help."

"Why does a ship need a carpenter?" Isis asked.

"I'll show you why," Silas replied. He carried the plank of wood over to a jagged hole in the side of the ship. "Hold this in place," he told them. "I'll get some nails."

Silas found some nails and started to hammer one in. "There's always stuff that needs repairing round here. This hole is where the *Revenge* took a hit from *Caroline's* cannonball." He chuckled. "If it wasn't for me, the ship would sink!"

Once the hole was patched, Tom helped Silas stuff strips of rope into the gaps between the new planks.

"This is called caulking," Silas said, hammering the rope into place with a mallet. He handed Isis a brush and pointed to a barrel of something black, sticky and stinky. "Now you've got to daub it with tar. Make it watertight, see?"

"Is there any treasure on board?" Tom asked, winking at Isis. Maybe Silas could give them some information about where to find the amulet.

Silas patted Tom's heads. "You're a funny lad!" he said. "As if I'd tell you!"

Isis offered Silas a rag so he could wipe his hands. "But say there *was* treasure on the ship, where would it be kept?" she insisted.

"Well, *if* there were treasure, it would be

in Blackbeard's cabin, of course!" Silas said, as he packed away his tools. "Safest place on the ship. I mean, who in their right mind would try robbing the captain's quarters? He locks it tight, and he even sleeps with a dagger, just in case."

Tom caught Isis's eye. *We've got to get into Blackbeard's cabin,* he thought. *We don't have a choice if we're going to get that amulet.*

"Are you asleep?" Isis whispered in the dark.

"No," Tom said. He lay swaying in his hammock, listening to the creaks and groans of the ship as it sailed through the rough seas. All round him, the sound of snoring had struck up, like a chorus of toads. Underneath the snores was a faint scurrying sound. Tom swung his legs over the side of his hammock and hopped silently to the ground, hoping to avoid any of the rats running along the deck. "Come on. It's time!"

Together, Tom and Isis clambered up to the moonlit main deck, where Blackbeard had his cabin.

Tom heard footsteps. He pulled Isis into the shadows, as the pirate who was standing guard strode by.

"Now!" Tom whispered.

They crept forwards, Cleo padding softly behind. With a thudding heart, Tom slowly turned the handle of the captain's door. It was locked — just like Silas had said it would be.

"Should we try to break it down?" Tom whispered to Isis.

"Don't be silly," Isis said. "Cleo will help us." Scooping up her pet cat, Isis held Cleo to the lock. With a few swipes of her claws, Cleo got it open.

Tom opened the door a crack and peered in, his heart pounding. Blackbeard was sound asleep, clutching a dagger in one hand.

Nodding to Isis, they slipped inside noiselessly. On a table, a candle was still burning and moonlight streamed through the porthole, filling the cabin with a dim light.

"Let's split up," Tom whispered, just loud enough to be heard above Blackbeard's snoring. "See if you can find any treasure."

Moving further into the cabin, Tom ran his fingers over a velvet sofa. Dangling from the ceiling above him was a chandelier.

This place is pretty grand compared to the rest of the ship, he thought.

Tom searched the fine oak shelves for a treasure chest. Nothing. He peered inside carved cabinets. Nothing. He even flipped up the rug, but there was no trapdoor underneath.

Suddenly, Blackbeard's voice rumbled through the darkness. "Have them flogged!" he shouted.

Tom froze. Isis glanced over at him with terror in her eyes. Had they been discovered?

Then, Blackbeard mumbled, "I don't want worm castles for tea, Mummy!"

Phew! Tom thought. *He's just talking in his sleep.*

Tom continued his search. On Blackbeard's desk, he found a map. He held it up to the light of the candle to get a better look. Isis joined him.

"It's a map of an island," Tom said, studying it carefully. There was a big black X marked near the north shore.

"Maybe that's where Blackbeard's buried the amulet," Isis said. "Should we take it?"

"That might make him suspicious. Let's just go – it doesn't look like there's any treasure in here."

But Cleo had other ideas... the playful little cat batted one of Blackbeard's shiny beard-ribbons, which were hanging over the side of the bed.

Tom quickly snuffed out the candle and pulled Isis into the shadows. Blackbeard sat bolt upright.

"Come out, whoever you are!" he growled.

He was definitely awake this time! Tom saw Blackbeard's dagger glinting in the moonlight. *How long will it take him to find us?* Tom wondered, trembling with fear.

Suddenly Cleo purred. She rubbed her fur against Blackbeard's bedding. There was a crackle of electricity. White sparks flew into the air.

"Aargh!" Blackbeard yelped. "What's that?"

It's static, Tom thought.

As if Anubis was helping them for once,

thunder rumbled and lightning flashed outside the porthole.

Blackbeard pulled the bed-sheets right up to his chest. He was shaking all over like a jelly. "St Elmo's Fiiiiiiire!" he wailed in a wobbly voice. Then he dived under the covers.

Tom grabbed Isis by the arm and, together with Cleo, they ran out of the cabin as fast as their legs would carry them.

CHAPTER 6
HOT CROSS GUNS!

As the sun rose over calm seas, Tom and Isis were helping Sal in the cramped galley. Sal was pouring grog into tankards.

"Show a leg, me heartie!" he said, ordering Tom to hurry up. "You don't want to cross a pirate with an empty stomach!"

Tom delved into the barrel of hard tack and pulled out enough weevil-infested biscuits for forty men.

"Go on! Ask Sal!" Isis hissed.

"Ask me what?" Sal said.

"Well, we were wondering if you know what St Elmo's Fire is," Tom said, piling the biscuits on to the tray that Isis was holding.

Sal started to slice up limes. "You two landlubbers don't know anything, do you?" he said, chuckling. "Well, I'm sure you've gathered that we pirates are a superstitious bunch?"

Tom and Isis nodded.

"We sailors believe that the purple and blue glow you get round the masts of a ship in a thunderstorm is a bad omen sent by our patron saint, Elmo."

"What rubbish!" Isis scoffed. "Everyone knows the Egyptian god Seth makes thunder and lightning happen."

Tom rolled his eyes.

"No pirate wants St Elmo's Fire on the

87

high seas!" Sal looked suddenly worried
and darted out of the galley, carrying
Blackbeard's breakfast tray.

Later, out on deck, Tom watched as
Blackbeard paced up and down the length
of the ship, muttering at anyone who got in
his way.

"Bad omens!" he bellowed at a young
pirate who was fixing the knots in some
rigging.

Blackbeard stomped off, kicking out at a
scrubbing brush that was in his path.

"Blasted brush! Think you can trip me
up and break my neck?!" he boomed.
"GGGGGRRRRR!" He picked up the
brush and threw it overboard.

Next, Blackbeard ordered an inspection.
The entire crew lined up, standing tall

with their guns slung across their chests. Blackbeard walked down the row, eyeing up every man from beneath bristly eyebrows.

Tom held his breath as the captain stopped in front of a short pirate. The colour drained out of the pirate's face. Blackbeard grabbed his gun and rubbed a tiny streak of oil off the barrel.

"Filthier than a bilge rat!" Blackbeard cried. "Little Jack!" he called to his quartermaster. "Give this backwards blowfish ten lashes o' the whip!"

As the offending pirate was dragged away, Tom gulped. *Blimey!* he thought. *If Blackbeard had caught us last night, imagine what sort of trouble we'd have faced!*

"Set sail for Coral Cove!" Blackbeard shouted. "We'll hide in the bay and watch the merchant ships sail past on their way

back to Europe."
He swung round
and grabbed
Tom and Isis by
their shirts. "Up
to the crow's
nest with you
two!" he said.
"I want you to
keep an eye out
for Spanish ships.
Big galleons.
White flag with a
knotted red cross.
Got it?"

"Yes," Isis
said, impatiently.
"Big ship,
red cross!"

Before Blackbeard could even say 'forty lashes', Isis had shinned up the mast. Tom followed close behind, leaving Blackbeard grumbling about St Elmo's Fire.

At the top, Tom stood on the opposite side of the crow's nest from Isis. He peered down at Blackbeard walking up and down the deck. The legendary pirate was looking out to sea through his telescope.

"So the red cross means we're looking for a Spanish ship, not a hospital," Tom said. "The riddle makes more sense now."

"I'm already bored," Isis said.

Tom looked out at the shipping lane. Blue sky. Blue sea. Four seagulls. "I know what you mean," he said. "If Blackbeard wasn't so scary, we could have a spitting competition!" He giggled mischievously.

"Yuck. You're such a disgusting boy!" Isis

said, wrinkling her nose. Then she grinned. "I'd definitely win that game!"

"Oh, let me guess," Tom said. "I bet you were trained at the age of four by the best spitter in your dad's army."

"Don't be ridiculous," Isis said, shaking her head. "I was trained by the best spitter in all of *Ancient Egypt*, silly!"

The two burst into fits of giggles.

Suddenly Isis stopped. "Ooooh! A ship!"

They watched as the tiny dot on the horizon sailed into view. The French flag was flying from the ship's mast.

"It's a French ship," Tom said, groaning. "No use to us. Let's keep a lookout"

The sun climbed high in the sky. Tom's legs ached after hours of standing in the cramped crow's nest. The heat was making him feel sleepy. First his head lolled forward.

92

Then his eyelids started drooping. But
suddenly he spotted something...

"A white flag with a red cross!" Tom
cried. He nearly fell out of the crow's nest
with excitement. He squinted at the galleon
bobbing in the distance. "Captain!" he called
down to Blackbeard. "Spaniards ahoy!"

Tom and Isis scrambled down to the deck.

"See how low in the water that ship is?"
Silas said, pointing at the galleon. "That
means its hold is full of cargo!" He lowered
his voice. "Rumour has it that this galleon is
carrying gold from Cuba!"

"Take down the Jolly Roger, men!"
Blackbeard barked, his eyes flashing. "Hoist
the Spanish colours. Let them think we're a
friendly vessel. Arrrr!"

The *Revenge*'s flag, with its warrior
skeleton and bleeding heart, was lowered.

93

"Below deck, men!" Blackbeard told the crew. "We don't want them seeing your ugly faces now, do we?"

Tom and Isis followed everyone to the hatch. They were just about to go down the stairs when—

"Not so fast, short stuff!" Blackbeard said.

Tom swung round to see the captain holding out two velvet dresses – one blue, one yellow – and feathered hats to match.

"Put these on!" he barked. "If the Spanish spot ladies on board, they'll think we're a harmless passenger ship. It tricks them every time!"

Isis grabbed the blue dress. She pulled it on straight away over her shirt and breeches. "Lovely!" she said, twirling. She took the fan that was sticking out from under Blackbeard's arm and started waving it about.

Tom shook his head. "I. Am. Not.

Wearing. A. Dress!" he said.

Then he noticed Blackbeard's fingers curl round the hilt of his cutlass.

"What I *meant* to s-say was, it looks j-just my colour," he said. Tom reached for the dress and quickly slipped it on.

"It's only fair," Isis said quietly, smoothing down her skirt. "After all, I've had to pretend to be a boy everywhere we've travelled to – now it's *your* turn to be girl."

Holding up his skirt, Tom stomped back and forth along the deck, scowling.

"You're meant to *stroll* like a lady not stomp like an elephant," Isis said, laughing.

Although Tom felt silly, he saw that Blackbeard's trick had worked. Thinking that the *Revenge* was another Spanish ship, the Spanish galleon sailed so close that its sails cast long shadows over Blackbeard's sloop. Tom read the name, *Santa Cruz*, on its prow.

Tom covered his face with his open fan so that nobody on the Spanish galleon would be able to read his lips. "Remember the riddle mentioned finding the amulet within sight of the red cross galleon?" he asked Isis. "Well, maybe the amulet…"

"Is on that ship!" Isis suggested.

"Send a warning shot, One-eye Pete!" ordered Blackbeard, peering out from his hiding place.

BOOM! The *Revenge* shook as the gunner fired the cannon at the *Santa Cruz*. The battle had begun!

CHAPTER 7
SUGAR, SPICE AND ALL THINGS NICE

"All hands on deck!" Blackbeard yelled. The pirates stormed up the stairs from below. Sal stepped on to the main deck, holding a wooden cooking spoon.

"You're going to want a better weapon than that, matey," laughed Blackbeard, as he strode past.

"Well I guess you're going to be a real pirate now, Sal," Tom said. "This is what you wanted, right?"

But instead of looking fierce and terrifying, Sal looked nervous.

Suddenly, realising it had been tricked, the *Santa Cruz* fired its cannon at the *Revenge*. The cannon ball missed and landed in the water with a splash, but the noise made Sal jump into action. He dropped his spoon, grabbed a sword and shouted, "Aaaaarrr!"

"That's more like it!" called Isis.

Tom watched as the Jolly Roger was raised. He wondered how the crew of the *Santa Cruz* would feel when they saw the skeleton holding the hourglass and spear. Would they realise straight away that it was the dreaded Blackbeard himself?! If they did, surely they would be terrified! He could see the oars of the Spanish galleon desperately trying to swing the giant ship round, but it was no use. The *Revenge* glided easily alongside it.

Blackbeard strutted up and down deck with his chest puffed out. "Throw those grappling hooks across! Pull them in!"

As soon as the galleon bumped up against the *Revenge*, Blackbeard leaped up on to the gunwale.

"Aaaaarrr! Prepare to be boarded, you Spanish rats!" he cried. He drew his cutlass

and jumped across on to the *Santa Cruz*'s deck. Firecrackers exploded beneath his hat. RAT-ATAT-TAT!

With a thudding heart, Tom watched as Sal and the other pirates started boarding the *Santa Cruz* with battle cries of, "Aaaaarrr!"

"Toss the grenades!" Blackbeard ordered the crew still on board, waving his cutlass in the air.

Suddenly, black egg-shaped missiles were pelted from the *Revenge*. They hit the deck of the *Santa Cruz*, bursting into clouds of smoke.

The Spanish crew were shouting and trying to fight off the pirates with their swords.

"What are you waiting for?" Isis asked Tom, grabbing a cutlass. She climbed up to the gunwale.

Tom's heart raced. He peered over at the struggle that was taking place on the *Santa Cruz*. *That looks bad*, he thought.

"Wait here for me, Fluffpot!" Isis called to Cleo. "I'll be back in a flash." She turned to Tom. "Well?" she asked. "Do you want to find the amulet or not?" Then she leaped across to the Spanish galleon.

"Here goes nothing!" Tom said, grabbing

another cutlass and following Isis over the gunwale, into the smoke and fighting.

The pirates' cutlasses clashed against Spanish swords. Fists flew. The Spanish sailors soon found themselves surrounded on all sides by Blackbeard's pirates and their deadly weapons.

As Tom and Isis hid behind two large barrels, Tom heard a growling voice through the smoke.

"Tell me where the gold is, or I'll pull your toenails off, one by one!"

Peeping between the barrels, Tom saw Blackbeard stooping over a man wearing a white wig, a large black hat and a tailcoat embroidered with gold.

Blackbeard held a knife to the man's throat. "Oro! Oro!" he bellowed. "That's your word for gold, isn't it, Capitán?"

The Spanish captain shook his head and kept his mouth tightly closed.

"Surrender, and we'll let you go," Blackbeard said, above the din of the fighting.

Tom nudged Isis. "We'd better hurry," he said. "Before the Spanish captain tells Blackbeard where the treasure is."

Isis pointed to a hatch at the far end of the deck. "Come on!" she said, pulling Tom through the smoke and dodging swords and cutlasses.

In the gloom of the hold, Tom and Isis rummaged through crates and barrels.

"There's lots of good things down here," Tom said, poking at a sack full of pale, sticky crystals. He tasted one. It was sweet. A barrel full of black goo was labelled 'Molasses'. "Sugar, spice and all things nice," Tom said.

"But no amulet," Isis said, sighing.
"Hurry! Let's check the captain's quarters."

They climbed some stairs, rounded a corner and *bam*! Tom and Isis ploughed headlong into a sailor who was guarding the door to the captain's room.

"Pirata!" the sailor cried in Spanish.

The young man drew his sword.

"Let's copy Blackbeard!" Tom whispered. "If we act terrifying enough, hopefully he'll surrender without a fight."

"Aaaaarrr!" Isis cried gleefully. She waved her cutlass in a frenzy.

Tom let out a deafening roar, held up his cutlass and pulled the scariest face he could think of.

Sure enough, the guard held up his hands, yelped and dropped his sword to the ground.

Tom grabbed some rope from a pile of

rigging and tied up the man's hands and feet, using knots that Silas had taught him. Then Tom and Isis pushed open the door grandly marked, "El Capitán."

Isis gasped and pointed to a treasure chest that was sitting on top of a fancy table. Embedded in its lid was a glittering blue amulet.

"There it is!" she said to Tom.

"Blackbeard's going to be down here faster than you can say *grog*," Tom said,

glancing at the door. "Let's get this chest out of sight so we can work the amulet free."

Tom and Isis managed to heave the heavy chest out of the captain's quarters and behind some rigging. They were just about to dig the amulet out when—

"Ooowww! Help!" cried a familiar voice.

Tom peered out from their hiding place. Sprawled on the deck, clutching his leg, was Sal. Blood poured from a nasty-looking gash in his thigh.

"Sal!" Tom said. "We've got to help him," he told Isis.

Isis nodded. She covered the treasure chest with a sail. "That should keep it hidden," she said. "We need to bind his wound."

Tom ripped strips of fabric from his gown. "Will this do?" he asked.

Isis nodded. "It didn't suit you, anyway,"

she chuckled. She started to wrap the cloth tightly round Sal's leg.

Sal moaned. "Shiver me timbers, I be in Davy's grip now," he said.

He grabbed Tom's hand and squeezed it so hard, Tom was fairly certain that his fingers would fall off.

As Isis tied the makeshift bandage, Tom saw fear in Sal's eyes. "Don't worry, you'll be all right," he said, then he and Isis helped Sal up to the top deck.

By now the battle was over. The Spanish sailors were sitting together, bound and gagged on the upper deck.

"Load that booty on to the *Revenge*, lads!" Blackbeard shouted to his men.

As fast as their legs could carry them, the pirates trundled up and down the stairs to the hold. Tom watched them carry barrels of

rum, crates full of sugar and spices, and rolls
of silk up from the galleon's hold and over a
ramp to Blackbeard's sloop.

Pretending to be looting, Tom and Isis
went back below deck. The sail was still

covering the most valuable thing of all. *Please don't let them find the treasure chest before we can get the amulet out*, he thought, crossing his fingers. *All we've got to do is wiggle it free with a dagger. Then we'll be home and dry!*

But suddenly the sound of Anubis's laughter echoed round the galleon.

"Don't think it's going to be that easy, boy!" the god of the Underworld boomed.

CHAPTER 8
THE CRAB'S CLAWS

"There must be a treasure chest lurking here somewhere!" Blackbeard shouted to his crew. "Find it!"

Just then, a blast of wind whipped up on board the *Santa Cruz*.

"Anubis!" Tom cried above the howling gust.

"If he weren't a god," Isis cried, "I'd tie his ears in a knot. See how he'd like that!"

Blackbeard stormed down the stairs. The

wind made his long beard flap over his face.

"What are you two standing idle for?" he shouted at Tom and Isis. "Get looking for the treasure before we're blown into the sea!"

As soon as the captain had spoken, the sail covering the treasure chest was picked up by the stiff wind. The treasure chest sat glittering on the deck. Just as quickly as Anubis's storm had blown up, it died down.

"Aaaaarrr! Treasure!" Blackbeard said, rubbing his hands. He stomped over to the chest, kneeled down and stroked the amulet. "My favourite thing in the world!"

Tom groaned. He turned to Isis. "You know what this means, don't you?" he whispered.

Isis nodded. "Looks like we're going to be pirates for a bit longer." She stroked her now-tattered dress and groaned. "Good job I like biscuits crawling with bugs."

With Blackbeard watching his crew's
every move, Tom and Isis helped the pirates
load the treasure chest on to the *Revenge*.
They walked along the plank between the
pirate ship and the Spanish galleon.

Blackbeard strutted up and down the

Santa Cruz's deck in front of the bound and gagged Spanish prisoners.

"As luck would have it, you Spanish rats," he said. "I'm going to let you go..."

The prisoners all sighed with relief.

"...all but one of you," Blackbeard said.

The prisoners looked at each other nervously and started to chatter in Spanish.

"Quiet!" Blackbeard shouted, waving his large silver pistol at them. "Who is the ship's doctor?"

A small man with a crooked grey wig raised his hand nervously.

Blackbeard pointed his pistol at the man. "Right, Señor Medico, you're coming with me! My own doctor got parrot fever, see? Ended up as fish food. Now the *Revenge* needs a medical man. So you'll do nicely! And bring all your supplies, too."

"*Si*," the Spanish doctor said as Blackbeard cut his bonds with his dagger.

Blackbeard pointed to Sal, whose bandages were now stained a dark red. "Take this lad to the infirmary," Blackbeard said.

The frightened-looking Spanish doctor straightened his wig, gathered his medical bag, and followed Blackbeard on to the *Revenge*. With the help of some of the pirates, the doctor carried Sal off to the infirmary.

Blackbeard stroked the lid of the treasure chest. "What you staring at, little shipmate?" he asked Tom.

"Er... I was admiring your leadership," Tom said, thinking quickly.

Blackbeard puffed out his chest and smiled. Then he looked up at the crow's nest of the *Revenge*. "Well, you can admire me from above," he said. "I need to find a good place to ground the ship." Blackbeard thrust his telescope into Tom's hand. "Up you both go!" he said, shoving Tom and Isis towards the mast.

"Anything?" Isis asked, yawning.

A cool breeze whipped round them as the pair stood in the crow's nest.

"I can see a strip of yellow," Tom said, squinting through the telescope. "It's definitely an island. Looks like..."

Isis leaned over the side of the crow's nest to get a better look. "A spider?"

"No. I'll give you a clue," Tom said. He pinched Isis on the arm.

"Ouch!" Isis squealed. "What was that for?"

"It was the clue," Tom said. "The island

looks like a crab!"

"Oh, yes!" Isis nodded. "Now you say it, it does look a bit crabby. And hang on, there was a crab in the riddle, wasn't there?"

"Exactly!" Tom said. "Something about 'pinching' the treasure from a crab. I bet that island is where we're meant to get the amulet!" His heart raced with excitement. "LAND HO!" he cried down to Blackbeard.

After the *Revenge* dropped anchor, Tom and Isis climbed down a rope ladder and waded to shore through the warm, shallow water. Tom splashed Isis.

"Hey!" Isis said. "You're getting me and Cleo all wet!"

"Back at the swimming pool you said you loved swimming," Tom said with a grin. "Now's your chance!"

"You're right," said Isis. She handed Cleo to Tom. "Look after Cleo while I have a paddle."

As Isis dived into the water, a yowling Cleo clung to Tom's head in terror.

Hmm, thought Tom, brushing Cleo's tail out of his eyes. *This wasn't exactly what I had in mind.*

While Isis floated on her back, Tom pointed over to the shore. "Hey! Look at Blackbeard!" he said.

The captain had already pitched a tent on Crab Island's beach under the shade of a palm tree. One-eye Pete and Silas were carrying the treasure chest inside. Blackbeard peered round suspiciously at his crew, then disappeared inside the tent.

"How are we going to get the amulet now?" Tom groaned.

There was no time to work out a plan. Tom and Isis were put to work helping

Little Jack share out the rum between the pirates.

"Go on, shipmate!" Little Jack said, thrusting a tankard of rum into Tom's hand. "You two get your fair share too!"

Tom remembered how disgusting the grog had tasted in the Jolly Barnacle Inn. "Er, no thanks. I'll give it a miss."

Isis wrinkled her nose. "Me too," she said.

"Suit yourself," Little Jack said. "All the more for me." And with that, he downed their share in just two gulps.

With their bellies full of warm rum, the pirates grew merry. One played a fiddle. One pulled out a concertina. One banged on a drum. Soon music filled the air and, as the sun went down, the pirates started to dance and sing shanties. They bellowed:

"*Oh, there once was a scurvy sea dog,*
Who fell into a barrel of grog…"

"I *love* dancing!" Isis said, wide-eyed with glee. She grabbed Tom's hand. "I'm a

brilliant musician. Let's join in!"

They were just about to dance a jig when Little Jack tapped them on the shoulder. "Not so fast, you two!" he said. "There's careening to be done. Get a knife and start scraping barnacles off the hull of the *Revenge*!"

"But I want to dance!" Isis cried, stamping her foot.

"Tough," Little Jack said. "If the *Revenge* is going to cut through the water quickly, she needs careening. And you two are going to do it."

The music and dancing carried on into the night. Tom looked down at the giant heap of barnacles. His hands were sore from scraping them off the ship. Cleo, at least, was happy. She was busy clawing out the sea creatures that lived inside the shells.

"This is rubbish!" Isis said. She threw her knife on to the sand. "It's too dark now to see anything."

"It could be worse," Tom said. "Just think about Sal."

"You're right," said Isis. "Let's go and pay him a visit to cheer him up."

They found Sal lying on a blanket in a tent with a few other injured pirates. His brow was sweaty. His injured leg was now a bandaged stump.

"Oh, Sal, I'm so sorry about your leg," Tom said, horrified.

"You poor thing!" Isis said.

Sal smiled and patted his stump. "Oh, I don't mind so much," he said. "Pirates get 800 pieces of eight for each limb they lose!"

"You get *paid* for your stump?" Tom asked.

Sal nodded. "Aye! It's the pirate code, matey!" Their friend looked suddenly serious. He cleared his throat. "Listen! Thank you for saving me back there... I would have died if it wasn't for you two." He patted Cleo gently on her fluffy head. "And you, little beauty... I'm sure you brought me and the *Revenge* luck!"

Sal needed to rest, so Tom and Isis said goodnight. The stars glittered like diamonds in the twilight. Pirates staggered about the beach, singing and fighting. Some were lying in the sand snoring.

But Tom only had eyes for Blackbeard's tent. "Now's our chance!" he whispered to Isis.

CHAPTER 9
GHOSTLY GAMES

"Right. How are we going to get past the guard?" Isis asked Tom, as she peered over at Blackbeard's tent.

Tom squinted through the dark. He could make out a spotted scarf, a mass of tangled hair and a pile of rags. The pirate was snoring loudly and clutching an empty tankard. "Looks like he's asleep. But if he wakes up, you'll have to distract him while I sneak past. Ask him to tell you about his most dangerous adventure, or something. Pirates love to show off."

Together, Tom, Isis and Cleo started to make their way across the beach. They ducked past three brawling pirates and tiptoed through another group, who were listening to One-eye Pete telling a scary story about the ghost of an angry octopus. Finally, all that stood between them and the tent were four tottering men, singing at the tops of their lungs:

"Shave his belly with a rusty razor,
Early in the morning!"

"Just walk past them," Tom whispered to Isis.

But one of the pirates grabbed Isis's hands and whirled her round in a drunken jig.

"Sing it with me, matey!" he growled. "This is me favourite shanty!"

"Aargh! Put me down, you toothless oaf! You smell like a pig's armpit!" she cried.

After two more verses of the shanty, Tom finally managed to pull Isis to safety. They slipped past the snoring guard and crept up to Blackbeard's tent.

"Let's hope he's nodded off too," Tom whispered, lifting the flap carefully. He peered inside... and breathed in sharply, dropping the tent flap shut again. Blackbeard was awake! He was sitting next to a flickering lantern, with the treasure chest in front of him, counting the gold.

Blackbeard jumped up, knocking over one of the gold stacks with a clank. Drawing his dagger, he snarled, "Who goes there?"

The captain burst through the opening of the tent. The blade of his dagger glinted threateningly in the moonlight.

Tom held his breath, terrified that the pirate would hear him.

"I'll slit your gizzard, so I will!" Blackbeard shouted. He paced back and forth in front of his tent, looking as though he was about to explode with anger, like one of his firecrackers.

When the captain went back into his
tent, Tom and Isis tiptoed across the sand as
quickly as they could.

"This is a disaster!" Tom whispered.
"We're no closer to getting that amulet.
We'd better think of something fast, or we'll
be stuck here forever!"

"I know you're out there,
you lily-livered scallywag!"
Blackbeard barked into the
night.

"Thinks he can scare me,
does he?" Isis whispered. She
sniffed. "Well, I've already
died once. He can't exactly
kill me again!"

That's it! Tom thought.
He tapped Isis on the arm.
"I've got a plan," he said,

breathless with excitement. "Follow me!" Running across the sand, he led Isis and Cleo to the moored bulk of the *Revenge*.

"Er... the amulet's back there, Professor Smartypants," Isis said, pointing her thumb in Blackbeard's direction. "Why are we over here?"

"You know how Blackbeard is really superstitious?" Tom explained. "Believing in all kinds of pirate hocus pocus, like the legend of Davy Jones's Locker and St Elmo's Fire..." He lowered his voice to a whisper as they passed a group of pirates sitting round a campfire toasting crabs on the ends of sharp sticks. "We're going to pretend to be ghosts and scare him!"

"That's a silly plan!" Isis scoffed.

Tom grinned at her. "No, it's not. *You* gave me the idea, anyway, when you said you had already died. Pirates are scared stiff of ghosts."

Isis stroked her hair. "In that case, *my* plan is *extremely* brilliant!"

Tom climbed on to the deck of the *Revenge* and grabbed a fishing rod. Next, they went back to the singing pirates. Most of them had fallen asleep, and Tom snatched up a flute lying in the sand.

"Do you know how to play this?" he asked Isis.

Isis ran her finger over the shiny silver flute. "Naturally," she said. She gave a little toot on the instrument. "I was one of the best musicians in the Nile Delta!"

Finally, Tom scooped up a handful of slimy seaweed, which Cleo swiped at.

"What are you doing, exactly?" Isis asked. "This is no time to go fishing."

131

Tom attached the seaweed to the hook on the end of the fishing rod. "You'll see. Ready for some fun?"

Outside Blackbeard's tent was a palm tree. Climbing up with the fishing rod tucked under his arm was tricky, but with some nifty footwork, Tom and Isis were soon perched at the top among the coconuts. Tom dangled the fishing line in front of the tent.

"We've got to get him to come back outside," he whispered to Isis. "Start playing something spooky."

Isis put the flute to her mouth and blew. Suddenly the flute came alive with the most haunting music Tom had ever heard. Cleo joined in with a wailing yowl. Before Tom could count to ten, Blackbeard flung back the flap and came out of the tent, dagger in hand.

"Who's there?" he called.

Tom tried to sound spooky.

"I am the ghooooost of the dread piiiirate, er, Bluebeard," he said in a trembly voice.

"I have come from Daaaaavy Jones's Lockerrr." He started to let out the fishing reel so the seaweed dangled lower and lower. "Ifffff you do not hand over the treasure chest, you'll be coming to staaaay with meeeeeee."

Next to him, Tom could feel Isis's shoulders shaking with silent laughter.

Blackbeard took a step forward into the dark night. Tom dragged the cold, slimy seaweed over the pirate captain's face.

Batting desperately at the seaweed, Blackbeard shrieked in horror. "Shiver me timbers!" he cried. "Ghosts! Bad omens! I'm doomed. Aaaaarrrgggh!" He dropped his dagger on to the sand. Waving his arms wildly, the pirate captain ran down the beach, as though Davy Jones himself was after him.

"Now's our chance!" Isis said. "Told you it was a brilliant plan!"

Tom, Isis and Cleo leaped down on to the sand and scrambled into the tent. Tom spotted the chest lying behind stacks of gold. He started to dig away at the amulet in the lid with the dagger Blackbeard had dropped. He wiggled and jiggled the blade. The blue amulet started to loosen and then – *pop!* – it flew right into Isis's hand.

"You did it!" Isis shrieked.

Together with Cleo, they ran out of Blackbeard's tent.

"All join hands," Tom said.

The blue amulet glowed and a fierce wind whipped round their legs. Tom closed his eyes as sand swirled into the air. Suddenly, the three travellers were caught in a time tornado. The beach became a blur, and the last thing Tom saw, before he was sucked up into the tunnels of time, was Blackbeard, running towards them, shaking his fist.

"You'll hang for this!" the pirate shouted.

CHAPTER 10
HOME AND DRY

As the trio shot out of the time tunnel, the smell of chlorine stung Tom's nostrils. He opened his eyes just in time to see water rushing up towards him.

"Aargh! Noooooo!"

Splash!

Tom did a painful bellyflop into the local swimming pool. When he surfaced, clutching his bright-red stomach, a whistle blew.

"Right, out you get, you lot!" the

swimming instructor shouted. "See you all
next week."

As Tom swam towards the steps, he saw
Isis and Cleo standing on the side of the
pool. They were once again wrapped in their
mummies' bandages.

"Well, we're back," Isis said. Looking
out of the window, she sighed. "And it's just
as rainy and gloomy here as ever, isn't it,
Fluffpot?" She clutched the mummified cat
close to her chest. "But at least now I've had
a swim. This pool's not quite the Caribbean
Sea, is it?"

Tom climbed out of the pool and grabbed
his towel from its peg. He was shivering from
the cold. His right ear was blocked with
water. "No," he chuckled, looking at the
section of the pool that was full of old ladies
in flowery swim caps doing an exercise class.

"It's not exactly a tropical paradise."

With wet hair dripping into his eyes, Tom walked into the boys' changing room. Isis and Cleo shuffled stiffly after him.

"Hey! No girls allowed," Tom said. Some of the boys from his class gave him strange looks as they hurried to get dressed.

"Oh, don't worry," Isis tutted. "Cleo and I will hide in one of the cubicles!"

"This amulet is gorgeous!" Isis said, pulling the door shut. "You know, it's exactly the same colour as the Caribbean Sea."

Shivering, Tom dried himself off and changed into his clothes. When all the other boys had left, Tom called out, "OK, Isis. You can come out now."

Isis opened the door and sat next to Tom on the bench. She stroked the amulet with her bandaged fingers.

"This goes so well with the colour of my skin, don't you think?" she cooed, holding the amulet up to her face.

"What skin?" Tom asked, stuffing his wet swimming gear into his bag. "You haven't got any, remember?"

A gust of wind suddenly blew up and all the locker doors started to bang open and shut.

"Here we go again!" Tom said.

Isis clung to the bench with both hands. The loose ends of her bandages fluttered out behind her. Cleo darted into a locker, arched her back and hissed.

"There's only one person who whips up a storm like this..." Isis yelped.

"Anubis!" Tom said.

Sure enough, Anubis burst out of a locker. First came his giant jackal's head – all black and snouty with red glowing eyes. Then came his huge man's body, seven feet tall and rippling with muscles.

With her paw, Cleo pulled the door of her locker firmly shut. "Meow!"

Anubis towered over Tom and Isis. He folded his arms and glared down at them. "Were you planning on giving me back my amulet?" he boomed at Isis.

Isis looked down at her toes. "Er..."

"Hand it over!" Anubis bellowed.

Isis plopped the glittering blue stone into the god's huge hand.

"Thanks for sending us on such a nice cruise," she said cheekily, tossing her head. "It was lovely to get some sun."

Tom gasped in horror. *No! Don't tease Anubis!* he thought.

Anubis leaned into Isis and blasted her with his stinky doggy breath. "Enjoyed yourself, did you?" he snarled. "It wasn't meant to be a holiday." He started to tap his bare foot on the changing-room floor. "Hmmmn," he growled. "It looks like I'm going to have to make the hunt for the sixth amulet MUCH more difficult."

"I didn't mean—" Isis began.

"It wasn't easy!" Tom interrupted.

"SILENCE!" Anubis shouted with a deafening bark.

Isis fell off the bench. Cleo yowled inside her closed locker. Tom hid behind the cubicle's door.

Anubis bared his teeth and twitched his
ears. "I'm surprised you two stupid children
have managed to find five of the amulets.

But believe me, the last amulet will be the hardest one to find yet." He turned to Isis and licked his jackal's muzzle. "And if you don't find it, you'll NEVER get into the Afterlife." He laughed nastily. "You'll be trapped in the gloomy Underworld FOREVER!"

There was a crack of thunder. Lightning flashed inside the changing room and Anubis vanished in a puff of smoke.

Tom realised he had been holding his breath for ages. He let out a big sigh of relief and stepped out of the cubicle.

"Phew! He's gone!" Tom said. "Now let's go home. I don't know about you two, but I need a snack that isn't wriggling with grubs!"

With his bag packed and Cleo and Isis stumbling along at his side, Tom thought about their latest adventure.

"Can you believe I almost went for a swim

with sharks in the Caribbean Sea?" he said, remembering how scary it had been to walk the plank. "And we lived on a pirate ship! How cool is that?"

"It wasn't cool," Isis said. "Those pirates were very smelly and sweaty. And that tub, the *Revenge,* was definitely not fit for a princess."

They stepped out of the leisure centre and into the drizzle. Tom pulled his jacket round him and thought longingly of the Caribbean sunshine.

"There aren't many people that can boast they've been real pirates!" Tom said. "It's the sort of thing most children dream of, you know?"

Isis suddenly stopped in the middle of a busy pavement, full of people hurrying on their way to and from the shops. Cleo looked up

at her mistress and cocked her head to
the side.

"What's wrong?" Tom asked.

Looking down, Isis sighed heavily.
"What if he's right, Tom?" she said in a
small voice. "What if I don't make it to
the Afterlife?"

Tom's fearless friend suddenly looked
frail and sad. His memories of being a
pirate slid to the back of his mind. He put
a reassuring hand on Isis's shoulder.

"Hey, come on!" he said. "Think of
all the amazing stuff we've done together.
All those adventures and challenges we've
had. No matter what Anubis has sent our
way, we've succeeded."

Isis looked up, but her head still drooped
slightly.

"We're a team, you, Cleo and me," Tom

said, taking his hand off her shoulder and wiping the dust off his fingers. "It doesn't matter where Anubis has hidden it, we'll find that sixth amulet! We're in it together. Right to the end, OK?"

Isis nodded. She picked up Cleo and gave her a cuddle.

"Anyway," Tom said. "We can't fail. If we did, I'd end up stuck with a mouldy old mummy and her cat forever!"

Tossing her head back and snorting, Isis said, "This mouldy old mummy adds a little excitement to your boring life, Professor Smartypants. You should be kissing my feet." She peered down at her toes. "On second thoughts, don't bother. I don't want my toes to fall off again. That stuff you call superglue isn't really that super."

Tom laughed and slung his bag over
his shoulder. He linked arms with Isis, and
the two of them strode off down the street,
singing,

"*Yo ho ho, hee hee hee,*
It's a pirate's life for me!"

TURN THE PAGE TO . . .

➜ Meet the REAL pirates!

➜ Find out fantastic FACTS!

➜ Battle with your GAMING CARDS!

➜ And MUCH MORE!

WHO WERE THE MIGHTIEST PIRATES?

Blackbeard was a *real* pirate. Find out more about him and other fierce pirates.

BLACKBEARD, whose real name was Edward Teach, was one of the most feared pirates of all time. Born in Bristol in 1680, Blackbeard terrified his enemies by wearing lit fuses in his thick black beard and daggers, pistols and a cutlass attached to his belt. The flag he flew on his boat, a ship he'd stolen and renamed the *Queen Anne's Revenge*, had a skeleton stabbing a heart. Yikes!

PIRATES
BLACKBEARD

Brain Power	300
Fear Factor	270
Bravery	345
Weapon: Cutlass	400

— TOTAL **1315** —

CAPTAIN WILLIAM KIDD was a privateer. Privateers were paid by a government to attack enemy merchant ships during wartime. Captain Kidd was asked by the king of England to attack French ships. But

PIRATES

CAPTAIN KIDD

Brain Power	190
Fear Factor	230
Bravery	220
Weapon: Dagger	160

— TOTAL **800** —

when his ship sailed past a navy yacht, the crew showed their bottoms instead of saluting. How rude! As punishment, Captain Kidd lost his crew to the navy. His new sailors were pirates who ignored his orders and attacked a British ship. In 1701, the British government hanged Captain Kidd for piracy. So remember – if you hang out with pirates, people will think you're one too!

HENRY MORGAN was a navy admiral who became a famous privateer. While the British and the Spanish were at war during the 17th century, the British government gave him permission to terrorise Spanish ships and settlements in the Caribbean. Morgan did so with great success and became very rich in the process. When the war between England and Spain ended, Morgan was having too much fun to stop – so he carried on! Spain was upset when he attacked

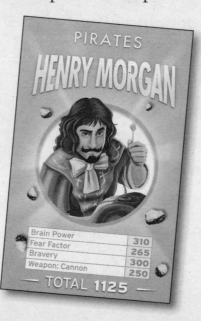

Panama, but King Charles II knighted Henry Morgan and made him deputy governor of Jamaica.

PIRATES

HENRY MORGAN

Brain Power	310
Fear Factor	265
Bravery	300
Weapon: Cannon	250
— TOTAL	1125 —

CALICO JACK

was a pirate whose real name was Jack Rackham. He got his nickname from the rough cotton clothes he wore. His flag featured a skull with two crossed swords –

the design we associate with pirate flags today – called the Jolly Roger. Calico Jack's swashbuckling crew included two women – his girlfriend Anne Bonny, and Mary Read, who tricked Calico Jack into thinking she was a man. Sneaky! In 1720, Calico Jack was captured by a pirate hunter and hanged in a Jamaican port, now called Rackham's Cay.

PIRATES
CALICO JACK

Brain Power	285
Fear Factor	220
Bravery	290
Weapon: Grenadoe	170

— TOTAL 965 —

WEAPONS

Blackbeard and his crew would attack and board other ships and then steal any valuables they found. Find out what weapons pirates used when they attacked.

Cannon: this would shoot iron balls 600–900 metres and needed four men to operate it.

Stinkpot: a clay pot filled with rotten fish or burning sulphur. It was thrown on to the deck during an attack so that it would smash, releasing gas that would overwhelm its victims and make them vomit.

Cutlass: a short, broad and slightly curved sword. Used in close hand-to-hand combat with an enemy.

Chain shot: two iron balls joined together by a thick chain. They were thrown across a ship's sails to damage them.

Grenadoe: an early hand grenade that is still used today. It was made from iron and filled with

gunpowder and sharp objects, and would explode when the fuse was lit.

CARIBBEAN PIRACY TIMELINE

In PIRATE MUTINY Tom and Isis stow away on a pirate ship!
During the 16th and 17th centuries piracy was common in
the Caribbean. Discover more in this brilliant timeline!

AD 1577
Queen Elizabeth I
recruits privateers
to attack Spanish
ships.

AD 1669
Henry
Morgan raids
Cuba.

AD 1701
Captain
William Kidd
is hanged for
piracy.

AD 1657
France and England
declare war on
Spain; privateering
grows in the
Caribbean.

AD 1700
Jolly Roger
flags start
to be used
widely on
pirate ships.

AD 1716–1730
After the war with Spain ends, unemployed privateers become pirates.

AD 1720
Calico Jack and his female crew members are captured.

AD 1715
New Providence in the Bahamas becomes a pirate base.

AD 1718
Blackbeard dies in battle.

AD 1820
American and British navies end piracy in the Caribbean.

TIME HUNTERS TIMELINE

Tom and Isis never know where in history they'll go to next!
Check out in what order their adventures *actually* happen.

3100 – 1070 BC
Ancient Egypt

300 BC – AD 476
Ancient Rome

776 – 323 BC
Ancient Greece

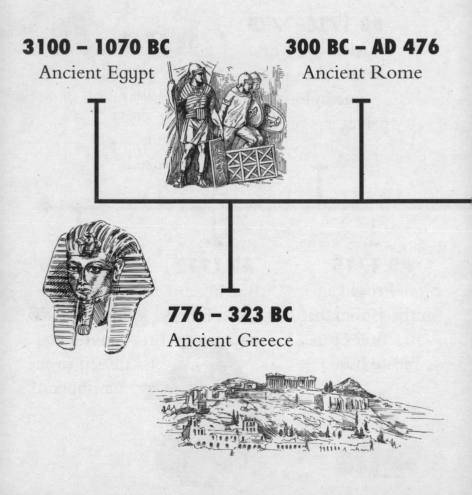

AD 1000 – 1300
Medieval England

AD 789 – 1066
The Age of the
Vikings

AD 1500 – 1830
Era of piracy in
the Caribbean

FANTASTIC FACTS

Impress your friends with these facts
about pirates.

➤ Pirates rarely made people
walk the plank. Instead, they
preferred other punishments, like
flogging people or leaving them
on a deserted island to starve.
That doesn't sound like a fun holiday!

➤ Pirates pierced their ears as they
believed that wearing silver and gold in them
would improve their
eyesight. *Wearing
glasses sounds less
painful!*

➤ Pirates wore eye patches as they often suffered from a disease called crickets that made them go blind in one eye. It was caused by a lack of vitamin C on long voyages. *Remember to eat your oranges!*

➤ Pirates thought it was acceptable to use an enemy's skull as a goblet to drink from, but it was rude to use it as a puppet to imitate the dead pirate. *Quite right too!*

➤ Only two privateers (no pirates) are recorded as having wooden legs and there is no historical evidence that any pirate ever owned a parrot. *Ohh-arrrr!*

WHO IS THE MIGHTIEST?

Collect the Gaming Cards and play!

Battle with a friend to find out which historical hero is the mightiest of them all!

Players: 2
Number of Cards: 4+ each

 Players start with an equal number of cards. Decide which player goes first.

 Player 1: choose a category from your first card (Brain Power, Fear Factor, Bravery or Weapon), and read out the score.

 Player 2: read out the stat from the same category on your first card.

→ The player with the highest score wins the round, takes their opponent's card and puts it at the back of their own pack.

→ The winning player then chooses a category from the next card and play continues.

→ The game continues until one player has won all the cards. The last card played wins the title 'Mightiest hero of them all!'

PIRATES
BLACKBEARD

Brain Power	300
Fear Factor	270
Bravery	345
Weapon: Cutlass	400
— TOTAL 1315 —	

For more fantastic games go to:
www.time-hunters.com

BATTLE THE MIGHTIEST!

Collect a new set of mighty warriors — free in every
Time Hunters book! Have you got them all?

GLADIATORS

- [ ] Hilarus
- [ ] Spartacus
- [ ] Flamma
- [ ] Emperor Commodus

KNIGHTS

- [ ] King Arthur
- [ ] Galahad
- [ ] Lancelot
- [ ] Gawain

VIKINGS

- [ ] Erik the Red
- [ ] Harald Bluetooth
- [ ] Ivar the Boneless
- [ ] Canute the Great

GREEKS

- ☐ Hector
- ☐ Ajax
- ☐ Achilles
- ☐ Odysseus

PIRATES

- ☐ Blackbeard
- ☐ Captain Kidd
- ☐ Henry Morgan
- ☐ Calico Jack

EGYPTIANS

- ☐ Anubis
- ☐ King Tut
- ☐ Isis
- ☐ Tom

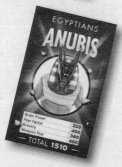

Who was King Tut?
How do you drive a chariot?
And what was an ankh?

Join Tom and Isis on another action-packed
Time Hunters adventure!

"You? Lead an army? What utter nonsense!"
General Horemheb scoffed. "You're far too
weak. You're an invalid, not a warrior!"

Tut looked at the floor and slumped his
shoulders.

Tom clenched his fists. "That's typical," he muttered. "Grown-ups always think they know best, even when they don't." He stepped forward, hands on his hips.

"Tut is a very fierce warrior, actually," Tom told the general. "And he can prove it!"

"I can?" Tut asked doubtfully.

Isis clapped him on the back. "Of course you can!" she said.

General Horemheb folded his thick, hairy arms over his leather tunic. "Very well," he said. His eyes narrowed. "If you can go hunting and bring back something big – and I mean really big, like a lion – then we'll know if you've got the skills and courage needed to lead an army in battle."

Then the general started to snigger. It was obvious to Tom that he didn't think Tut could complete the task, or lead an army.

Tut gulped. "Right. I will then!" he said in a shaky voice.

You can, Tut! Tom thought. *You really can!* He knew that Tut didn't believe he could succeed, but luckily the pharaoh had Tom and Isis to help him. It wasn't going to be easy to turn the boy-king into a fierce warrior – but no challenge had ever stopped them before!

"Cheer up, boys! I've seen camels look happier than you two," Isis said to Tom and Tut as they climbed into Tut's chariot. "Tutty Boy here is going to be a big success!"

Tom looked at Tut, who was getting tangled up in his bow and quiver full of arrows. "Do you really think so?" King Tut asked.

"Of course," Isis said, winking. "You've

got a brilliant teacher — me!"

Tut shook the reins and the horses pulled the chariot slowly out of the palace grounds. Before long, the horses picked up speed. Tom closed his eyes and enjoyed the wind whipping through his hair as they raced towards the dry, sandy desert.

"I'm going to be terrible on the battlefield," Tut said, sighing. "How can I fight with my bad leg? Maybe General Horemheb was right — I'm not strong enough to be a warrior king."

"Strength isn't the only thing a warrior needs," said Tom. "Brains and bravery are just as important." He thought back to all the opponents he and Isis had fought — powerful pirates, vicious Vikings, and great big gladiators. Even though they were much smaller, Tom and Isis had defeated them all.

"Listen, as long as you can use your bow and arrow, you'll be fine," Isis said. "Plus, you've got a fantastic chariot – it's a great ride."

As they flew over the rocky ground, Tom had to agree – riding in a chariot was even more fun than he could ever have imagined. He'd happily trade his bike for one any day!

"You don't need to be the fastest sprinter in Egypt to be a great pharaoh," Isis continued. "But you do need to be a good hunter if you're going to win the respect of your people. So I'm going to teach you how."

Tut raised an eyebrow at her. "You seem to know an awful lot about being a pharaoh."

Isis giggled. "Natural wisdom," she said.

Before long, the dry plains ended and the path became lined with long grass and trees.

Tut reined in the horses and the chariot came to a halt near a large tree.

"Pass me your bow and arrow," Isis told Tut. "I'll teach you how to use them."

Isis walked fifty paces away from the tree. "Target practice," she explained. "Tut, you'll start here and then move further away as you get better."

She nocked an arrow and fired it straight into the trunk of the tree. It hit the target with a satisfying thwack. Isis grinned.

"You're such a good shot!" Tut said, clearly impressed.

"My father taught me," Isis explained. "He was an expert hunter. And soon you will be too."

THE HUNT CONTINUES...

Travel through time with Tom and Isis as they battle the mightiest warriors of the past. Will they find all six amulets, or will Isis be banished from the Afterlife forever? Find out in:

Got it! ☐

Got it! ☐

Got it! ☐

Got it!

Got it!

Got it!

Tick off the books as you collect them!

TIME HUNTERS

Go to:

www.time-hunters.com

Travel through time and join the hunt for the mightiest heroes and villains of history to win **brilliant prizes!**

For more adventures, awesome card games, competitions and thrilling news, scan this QR code*:

*If you have a smartphone you can download a free QR code reader from your app store